W9-ATZ-257

LET'S GO
IN THE
FUNNY ZONE

Jokes, Riddles, Tongue Twisters & "Daffynitions"

By Gary Chmielewski

Illustrated by Jim Caputo

Read Jokes. Write Jokes.

A Note to Parents and Caregivers:

As the old saying goes, "Laughter is the best medicine." It's true for reading as well. Kids naturally love humor, so why not look to their interests to get them motivated to read? The Funny Zone series features books that include jokes, riddles, word plays, and tongue twisters—all of which are sure to delight your young reader.

We invite you to share this book with your child, taking turns to read aloud to one another, practicing timing, emphasis, and expression. You and your child can deliver the jokes in a natural voice, or have fun creating character voices and exaggerating funny words. Be sure to pause often to make sure your child understands the jokes. Talk about what you are reading and use this opportunity to explore new vocabulary words and ideas. Reading aloud can help your child build confidence in reading.

Along with being fun and motivating, humorous text involves higher order thinking skills that support comprehension. Jokes, riddles, and word plays require us to explore the creative use of language, develop word and sound recognition, and expand vocabulary.

At the end of the book there are activities to help your child develop writing skills. These activities tap your child's creativity by exploring numerous types of humor. Children who write materials based on the activities are encouraged to send them to Norwood House Press for publication on our website or in future books. Please see page 24 for details.

Above all, the most important part of the reading experience is to have fun and enjoy it!

Sincerely,

Shannon Cannon

Shannon Cannon
Literacy Consultant

NORWOOD HOUSE PRESS

P.O. Box 316598 • Chicago, Illinois 60631
For information regarding Norwood House Press, please visit our website at: www.norwoodhousepress.com or call 866-565-2900.

Designer: Design Lab
Project Management: Editorial Directions

Library of Congress Cataloging-in-Publication Data:
Chmielewski, Gary, 1946–
  Let's go in the funny zone : jokes, riddles, tongue twisters &
daffynitions / by Gary Chmielewski ; illustrated by Jim Caputo.
      p. cm. — (The funny zone)
  Includes bibliographical references and index.
  Summary: "Book contains 100 transportation-themed jokes, tongue twisters and 'Daffynitions'. Backmatter includes creative writing information and exercises. After completing the exercises, the reader is encouraged to write their own jokes and submit them for future Funny Zone titles. Full-color illustrations throughout"—Provided by publisher.
  ISBN-13: 978-1-59953-182-3 (library edition : alk. paper)
  ISBN-10: 1-59953-182-8 (library edition : alk. paper) 1.
Transportation—Juvenile humor. I. Caputo, Jim, ill. II. Title.
PN6231.T694C46 2008
818'.5402—dc22   2007045537

Manufactured in the United States of America

GETTING AROUND

What do you call a merry-go-round for ghosts?
A scareousel!

Knock, knock.
Who's there?
Rhoda.
Rhoda who?
Rhoda horse all the way through Texas!

What did the first stoplight say to the second stoplight?
"Don't look, I'm changing!"

What do you call Rollerbladers who chat on the computer?
Online skaters!

Why was the wheel such an important invention?
It got everything else rolling!

What meal helps drivers to avoid accidents?
Brakefast!

Did you hear about the tire that had a nervous breakdown?
It couldn't handle the pressure!

Why did the old woman tie skates on the rocking chair?
She wanted to rock and roll!

A horse is tied to a 20-foot-long rope. The horse wants to get some oats that are 30 feet away. The horse gets the oats easily. How is this?
The other end of the rope isn't tied to anything!

What goes up and down without moving?
Stairs!

What does a witch say to her broom before she goes to bed?
"Nighty night and sweep tight!"

What is the hardest thing about learning to roller skate?
The ground!

Traveler: "I'd like to buy a round-trip ticket."
Ticket Agent: "To where?"
Traveler: "Back to here, of course!"

Who's the fastest witch?
The one that rides on a Vrroooom stick.

5

ON THE ROAD

What goes best with toast when you're in a car?
Traffic jam!

During which school period do cars get put together?
Assembly!

Don: "I've never had a problem with backseat driving, and I've been driving for over twenty-five years!"
James: "What kind of car do you drive?"
Don: "A hearse!"

How do small children travel?
In mini vans!

Harvey: "You sure take your car in for a lot of repairs."
Bobby: "I know, my dad is always braking it!"

What did one windshield wiper say to the other windshield wiper?

"Isn't it a shame we seem to only meet when it rains?"

What ten-letter word starts with g-a-s?

Automobile!

THE CARGO
What gasoline makes.

Why is an old car like a baby?

They both have rattles!

What kind of man is strong enough to hold up a car with one hand?

Which snakes are found on cars?
Windshield vipers!

What part of a car is the laziest?
The wheels — they're always tired!

What kind of music do drivers listen to?
Car-tunes!

Jerry: "My older brother crashed his car into a tree going over 40 miles an hour."
Laura: "Wow! I didn't know a tree could move that fast!"

What do you get when you cross an automobile with a household animal?
A carpet!

When driving through fog, what should you use?
Your car!

What driver doesn't have a license?
A screw driver!

What kind of cars do ghosts drive?
Boo-icks!

What did the jack say to the car?
"Need a lift?"

Who drives away all of his customers?
A taxicab driver!

Why did the man put his car in the oven?
He wanted a hot rod!

Why did the man have to fix the horn of his car?
Because it didn't give a hoot!

What is white, has a horn, and gives milk?
A dairy truck!

Where do you find roads without vehicles?
On a map!

What has wheels and flies, but is not an aircraft?
A garbage truck!

What happens when a frog's car breaks down?
It gets toad away!

Where does a ghoul refuel his car?
At a ghastly station.

What do you call cars in the fall?
Autumn-mobiles!

CARNATION
A country where everyone owns a car.

Policeman: "Stop! This is a one-way street!"
Jim: "Well, I'm only going one way!"
Policeman: "Yes, but everyone else is going the other way!"
Jim: "Well, you're a policeman, make them turn around!"

Customer: "I've come to buy a car, but I don't remember the model. All I know is that it starts with 'T.'"
Salesman: "Sorry. We don't have any cars that start with tea. All our cars start with gas!"

"This is a magic car," said Lupita as she gave the keys to her daughter.
"Really?" exclaimed the excited teenager.
"Yes," said Lupita. "One speeding ticket and it will disappear!"

Knock, knock.
Who's there?
Cargo.
Cargo who?
Cargo beep-beep.

The police station received a call.
"Someone just stole my new car!"
"Did you see who it was?" asked the duty sergeant.
"No, but I got the license number," replied the caller.

TWO-WHEELING

**What did the skeleton say
while riding his motorcycle?**
"I'm bone to be wild!"

Do old bikers ever die?
No, they just get recycled!

Dad: "Javier, why did you let the air out of the tires on your bicycle?"
Javier: "So I could reach the pedals!"

Teacher: "Does anyone know what it means to recycle?"
Jennifer: "That's when I have to ride my older sister's bicycle instead of getting a new one!"

Mother: "Marcus, why aren't you sharing your scooter with your little brother?"
Marcus: "I am, Mom, half and half. I use it on the way down the hill, and he has it on the way up the hill!"

WATER, WATER EVERYWHERE

A submarine pilot was asked,
"How's business?"
He replied: "It has its ups and downs!"

HEROES
What a guy does to make
the boat move!

Where do spooks go sailing?
Lake Eerie!

When is a boat cheapest?
When it's a *sale* boat!

15

What kind of crew does a monster ship have?
A skeleton crew!

A boat racer was asked,
"How's business?"
She replied: "Sails are rising!"

What bus crossed the ocean?
Christopher Columbus in 1492!

Where do sick boats go?
To the dock!

What kind of lettuce did they serve on the Titanic?
Iceberg!

What do you throw out when you want to use it, but take in when you don't want to use it?
A boat anchor!

How do vampires travel the ocean?
By blood vessel!

How often do ships sink?
Only once!

Tooth Ferry
What you get when you cross a dentist and a boat.

ROOT CANAL

The Rinse & Spit

Swim-Ins Welcome!

Open 9 to 5pm

Why didn't the opera singer get a job on the cruise ship?
She was afraid of the high Cs!

What do you call the two owners of a sea-going vessel?
A partnership!

What part of a ship is always tired?
The pooped deck!

What did the ship say when asked what time it wanted to sail?
"The schooner the better!"

UP IN THE SKY

What did the ocean say when a plane flew over?
Nothing. It just waved!

Why was the airplane pilot fired?
Because of all the days he took off!

An air traffic controller was asked, "How's business?" She replied: "Can't come, plane!"

The flight attendant was taking orders. She asked one woman, "Would you like a meal?" "What are my choices?" asked the woman. "Yes or no," replied the attendant.

Why were the inventors of the airplane correct in thinking they could fly?
Because they were the Wright brothers!

Why did the student do her homework in an airplane?
She wanted to have a higher education!

Why do they always show bad movies on an airplane?
The audience can't walk out in the middle!

What's a ghost's favorite form of transportation?
Scareplane!

What happens when a witch flies faster than her broom?
She goes flying off the handle!

BY RAIL

What kind of ears do trains have?
Engin*ears*

What goes all the way from New York to Chicago without moving?
Railroad tracks!

Which car on the train snores?
The sleeping car!

Chew-Chew Train
A train loaded with bubble gum.

What's the best type of shoes to wear at the train station?
Platform shoes!

TRACK 29

GROOVY BABY

DISCO FEVER

FAR OUT!

How do you find a lost train?
Follow its tracks!

What did the engineer say when he saw the new locomotives?
"Diesel be fine!"

Two twin trains travel twisted tracks.

BIG FOOT

If you were standing directly on Antarctica's South Pole facing north, which direction would you travel if you took one step backward?
North – all directions from the South Pole are north!

While walking across a bridge, I saw a boat full of people. Yet on the boat there wasn't a single person. Why?
Everyone on the boat was married!

The more of them you take, the more you leave behind. What are they?
Footsteps!

What walks all day on its head?
A nail in a horseshoe!

WRITING JOKES CAN BE AS MUCH FUN AS READING THEM!

Riddles are one of the most popular kinds of jokes. They are usually a short question followed by a short answer. Some riddles are puns (jokes based on words that have two meanings or two words that sound the same but have different meanings). Other riddles show a different way to look at a person, place or thing. Here is a riddle from page 6:

What goes best with toast when you're in a car?
Traffic jam!

To understand this joke, you have to know that "jam" is a fruit spread that you put on toast. You also have to know that when you pair the word "jam" with the word "traffic," it means that a street or highway is filled with cars and traffic isn't moving very quickly.

Go back and re-read the jokes in this book. Which of them are riddles? Which ones do you think are funny? Try to figure out what makes them so funny.

YOU TRY IT!

You can do this joke-writing exercise by yourself or with a group of friends. Pick a form of transportation (for example: car, airplane, train, etc.). Next, brainstorm as many words as you can think of that are related to that form of transportation. Don't stop to think about whether the words would be good for writing riddles, just list everything that comes to mind.

After you have a list of words that are related to your form of transportation, use the words to write a few riddles about it. If you're working with friends, have everyone take a turn coming up with a riddle. Write down all the riddles.

Test out your jokes on friends or family members who haven't heard them yet. Did they laugh? If you answered yes, congratulations! You are now an official joke writer!

SEND US YOUR JOKES!

Pick out the best riddle that you created and send it to us at Norwood House Press. We will publish it on our website — organized according to grade level, the state you live in, and your first name.

Selected jokes might also appear in a future special edition book, *Kids Write in the Funny Zone*. If your joke is included in the book, you and your school will receive a free copy.

Here's how to send the jokes to Norwood House Press:

1) Go to www.norwoodhousepress.com.
2) Click on the **Enter the Funny Zone** tab.
3) Select and print the joke submission form.
4) Fill out the form, include your joke, and send to:

The Funny Zone
Norwood House Press
PO Box 316598
Chicago, IL 60631

Here's how to see your joke posted on the website:

1) Go to www.norwoodhousepress.com.
2) Click on the **Enter the Funny Zone** tab.
3) Select **Kids Write in the Funny Zone** tab.
4) Locate your grade level, then state, then first name.
    If it's not there yet check back again.